R.A. SALVATORE'S

DemonWars™

TRIAL BY FIRE

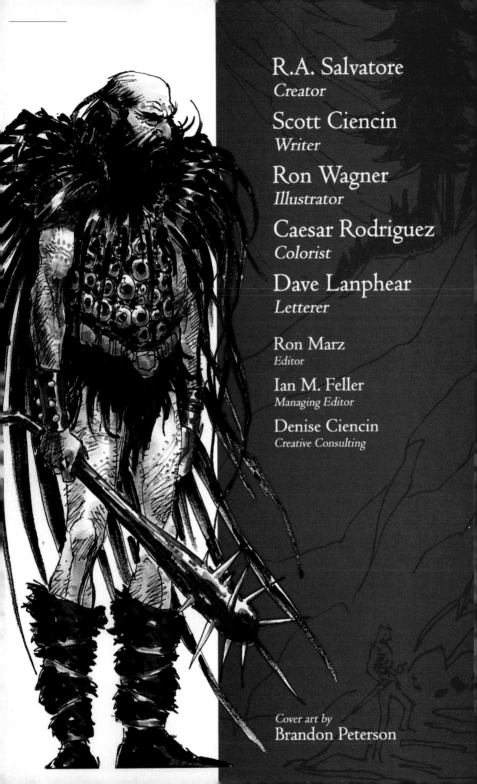

R.A. Salvatore
Creator

Scott Ciencin
Writer

Ron Wagner
Illustrator

Caesar Rodriguez
Colorist

Dave Lanphear
Letterer

Ron Marz
Editor

Ian M. Feller
Managing Editor

Denise Ciencin
Creative Consulting

Cover art by
Brandon Peterson

R.A. SALVATORE'S
DemonWars

TRIAL BY FIRE

INTRODUCTION BY
R.A. SALVATORE

The widening of the world of *Demon Wars* is well underway now, and even though I was determined to do this — to get other creative people into the process of expanding the world — I have to admit that I held my breath at the beginning of "Trial by Fire."

I'm breathing a lot easier now. The storytelling, both with words and images, has been amazing. I truly feel that Corona is a better place because of the work of Scott Ciencin, Ron Wagner and all the others.

CrossGen wanted me to write an Andacanavar story for this collection. It made sense, since he's the tie to the novels. However, after reading the five comics, I wanted something else. I called Scott Ciencin and asked for his permission to use Grave Mungo as my main character! I also asked him to be the front-end editor on the story. You'll see the result inside.

So far, this is everything I had hoped it would be, and more. Not only has this series expanded the world and made it more vibrant, but Scott has given us one of the more unforgettable characters I've seen in a long time.

−R.A. Salvatore

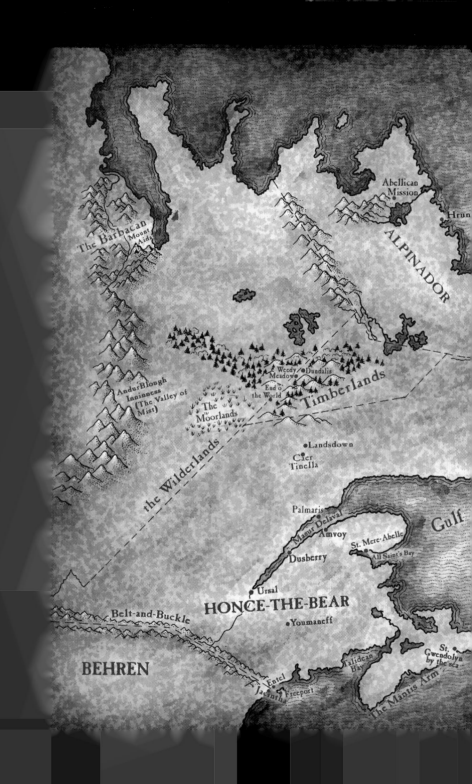

THE WORLD OF
CORONA

THE
JULIANTHES

(The Weathered Isles)

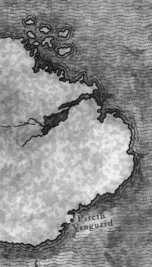

Pireth
Vanguard

of
Corona

Pireth
Dancard

MIRIANIC

OCEAN

Pireth
Julme
Tinson

Macomber

The Broken Coast

N

TRIAL BY FIRE • CHAPTER ONE

"COME, DEMON..."

...TASTE *STEEL* FORGED IN HATE OF YOUR KIND.

COME AND BE *DAMNED* BY THE WILL OF DANE THORSSON!

CAPTAIN, WE'RE *OVERRUN!* OUR ONLY ESCAPE IS THE *SEA!*

NEVER.

I'LL LOOK *DEATH* IN THE EYE AND GO TO THE AFTERLIFE IN *HONOR...*

"BORROK NEENOCH, MY LEADER, THE WAY THAT ONE FIGHTS...

"...IT IS THE BI'NELLE DASADA...

"...THE ELVEN SWORD DANCE."

"AYE, GREMPH, AND HIS SWORD...

"...THAT'S SILVEREL. AN ELVEN BLADE."

BY THOSE WHO LIE BELOW... STRATEGIC WITHDRAWAL!

RUN AWAY!

WARRIOR, WHAT IS YOUR NAME?

I'M ANDACANAVAR. THE RANGER.

DEMON.

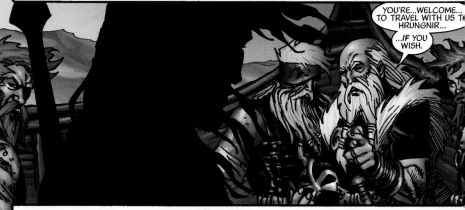

YOU'RE...WELCOME... TO TRAVEL WITH US T HRUNGNIR...

...IF YOU WISH.

AYE. I'LL DO THAT.

MY THANKS.

DEAL! I'LL SEE THEM DEAD! **ALL DEAD!**

OR MAYBE I CAN FIND SOMETHING VALUABLE TO THEM, AND **TAKE** IT...

...AND THEIR RICHES, **ALL** THEIR RICHES, WILL BE THE RANSOM...

...THEN WE'LL FIND THEIR HOUSES AND **BURN 'EM** ALL!

PAY ATTENTION, RUNT!

RIGHT. PLUNDER AND REVENGE.

THAT'S THE WAY TO GO. I MEAN, **THEY** STARTED IT, AFTER ALL, NOW DIDN'T THEY?

BORROK NEENOCH HEARS YOU, GRAVE MUNGO. JUST TAKE CARE OF WHAT YOU **SCAVENGED** FROM THE DEAD.

AND **WATCH YOURSELF.**

Ah, SIR...WHAT'S HE SUPPOSED TO WATCH HIMSELF DOING?

WHY COULDN'T YOU HAVE **DROWNED,** GREMPH?

"WATCH MYSELF."

EVEN THE **DEAD** MUST HAVE IT BETTER THAN THIS.

21

"...EYES LIKE *FIRE*... SKIN BLACK...CHARRED...

"...VEINS LIKE GLOWING *LAVA*... THE TEETH...AND CLAWS...WHY..."

...WHY DID IT ONLY *WOUND* US?

WHY NOT KILL US AND BE DONE WITH IT?

A MOMENT, TRAVELER...

I AM **ABBOT GREENE**, AND WE OF THE **ABELLICAN** FAITH HAVE TRAVELED FAR TO SHOW YOU **WONDERS**.

LOOK UPON THE MAGICAL GEMSTONES OUR ORDER HAS THE **SACRED DUTY** TO PROTECT.

AMONG THEM ARE STONES WITH THE POWER TO HEAL EVEN THE MOST **TERRIBLE** WOUNDS.

BUT THIS POWER WON'T BE USED ON **UNBELIEVERS**. IF YOU WISH TO BE HEALED...

...YOU MUST RENOUNCE YOUR PRIMITIVE GODS AND **GIVE YOURSELF** TO OUR FAITH.

OTHERWISE...

...HONESTLY, I DOUBT MANY OF YOU WILL **SURVIVE**.

LYING **WITCH**!

DON'T **TOUCH** ME! I WON'T BECOME A **DEMON**! YOU WON'T HAVE MY **SOUL**!

BUT—

YOU ARE THE HERETICS! THE GOD YOU WORSHIP IS A **LIE**!

THOSE STONES...

...**ALL MAGIC** IS EVIL. WE'D RATHER SUFFER AND **DIE** THAN RISK OUR SOULS!

ABBOT, WE MUST **TEACH** THEM. THEY MUST KNOW THAT MAGIC **ISN'T** GOOD OR EVIL, IT'S THE HAND **WIELDING** IT THAT MAKES THE DIFFERENCE.

AND THAT THE HEALING STONES **DON'T** TAKE YOUR SOUL, THAT'S JUST A TALE–

ENOUGH.

IT'S TIME FOR THOSE TRUE TO THE **FAITH** TO ADJOURN FOR SERVICES.

AS FOR THE REST OF YOU, IT'S WARM AND **SAFE** WITHIN.

ANY WHO CHANGE THEIR MINDS...

...AND FEEL STRONG ENOUGH TO **CRAWL TO THE DOOR**...

...ARE WELCOME TO **JOIN** US.

NO...

DEAR SISTER MOIRA... YOU SEEM *TROUBLED*.

THE COURTYARD IS OPEN TO THE *OUTSIDE*, THOSE PEOPLE–

ARE PERFECTLY *SAFE*.

WARDS HAVE BEEN ERECTED TO PREVENT *WHATEVER* HARMED THEM FROM EVEN *APPROACHING* THE MISSION.

ABBOT, WE COULD HAVE PASSED OFF OUR MAGIC AS NATURAL HEALING, AS WE OFTEN DO WITH UNBELIEVERS. THERE WAS *NO* REASON–

THERE WAS *EVERY* REASON. WE ARE IN ALPINADOR TO *CONVERT* FOLLOWERS.

ONE OF THESE WRETCHES *WILL* CONVERT, THEN SPREAD THE WORD TO OTHERS.

OR PERHAPS IT WILL BE ONE OF THE *NEXT* LOT.

THEY *WILL* COME AROUND. THEY ALWAYS *DO*.

...THE *NEXT* LOT...

YOU'RE OUT THERE, WHATEVER YOU ARE. JUST *WAITING*...

WE CAN'T GET PAST THE *WOODS* TO WARN OTHERS TO STEER CLEAR, AND THOSE PEOPLE YOU'VE *HURT* CAN'T GET AWAY TO FIND HEALERS THEY'LL *TRUST*.

I THINK WE SHOULD *TALK* ABOUT THAT...

...*JUST* THE TWO OF US.

Ah, BUT SHE LED ME ON A **MERRY** CHASE!

A **GIANTESS**, SHE WAS, A SAVAGE **BEAST** RIPE FOR THE SLAUGHTER!

MY BLADE, DIPPED IN **POISON**, BROUGHT HER LOW.

"PLEASE, NO!" SHE CRIED, HOWLING WITH PAIN. *"LET ME GO TO MY HUSBAND, I AM WITH CHILD!"*

"HAH! HIDEOUS THING," I TOLD HER, *"IF YOU HAVE A CHILD WITHIN YOU, IT'S LIKELY BECAUSE YOU ATE ONE OF OURS!"*

SHE **GASPED** AS MY SWORD FLASHED, TAKING HER LIFE...

...AND HER **HEAD!**

HAHAHAHAHAHAHA

AYE, CHIEFTAIN BYGGVIR!

SLAUGHTER **ALL** THE DEMONS!

WHAT'S *YOUR* PROBLEM, DAINTY HAIR? NO TASTE FOR *GLORY* AND GREAT DEEDS?

OR DOES THE SIGHT OF *BLOOD* MAKE YOU PALE?

=HHHH=

WHUD

THUNK

HUH. FOR AN *ALPINADORAN*, HE'S NOT MUCH FOR HOLDING HIS MEAD, NOW *IS* HE?

HAHAHA HAHAHA HA

ANDACANAVAR, TELL ME OF YOUR YEARS *AWAY* FROM ALPINADOR. I'VE SEEN *NOTHING* SAVE THIS FROZEN LAND. BUT *YOU...*

I'VE HEARD IT SAID THAT YOU WERE RAISED BY THE *ELVES*, THAT YOU'VE TRAVELED THE WORLD, SEEN *MAGIC* AND *WONDERS.*

I, AH... ...ON THE MORROW, I'M *FINALLY* VISITING THE ABELLICAN MISSION.

THERE ARE SO MANY THINGS I WANT TO SEE, BUT IT SEEMS *IMPOSSIBLE...*

ALL THINGS ARE POSSIBLE. ALL THINGS ARE *TRUE.*

YOU JUST NEED TO MASTER THE RIGHT WAY OF LOOKING AT LIFE, ELENE, PERHAPS AS AN *ARTIST* MIGHT.

MY ART IS WITH THE BLADE. WHAT *FOOLISHNESS* IS THIS HE PUTS IN ELENE'S HEAD, CHIEFTAIN?

I'LL CUT OUT HIS *HEART* IF HE TEMPTS MY DAUGHTER TO STRAY BEYOND OUR BORDERS!

RANGER. A WORD, IF I MAY...

UNDERSTAND ME, DEMON. YOUR PRESENCE HERE IS TOLERATED *ONLY* BECAUSE YOU ARE ALPINADORAN BY BLOOD, AND BLOOD TIES ARE SACRED TO US.

BUT I'LL *NOT* HAVE YOU DRIVE MY DAUGHTER EVEN FURTHER AWAY FROM ME WITH SUCH TALK. I'LL SEE *YOUR* SKULL ON THIS WALL FIRST.

YOU CAN'T WALK IN *TWO WORLDS,* ANDACANAVAR. YOU HAVE TO CHOOSE.

I MADE MY CHOICE A *LONG* TIME AGO.

COME, LIGHTNING.

THE RIDE WILL TAKE THE *NIGHT,* BUT PERHAPS THE HEARTH OF THE *ABELLICANS* WILL BE A SHADE MORE WELCOMING...

"MURDERERS..."

...THIEVES!

GRAVE, YOU WORTHLESS FOOL, GRAB THE GIRL!

...RIGHT, THANKEE, THANKEE, NEVER WOULD HAVE OCCURRED TO ME, IT'S ONLY THE ENTIRE PLAN, KIDNAP AND RANSOM THE CHIEFTAIN'S DAUGHTER...

...MORON...

Oh.

PROTECT ME.

PLEASE.

YWEEEH!

NO...

WHY *NOT?*

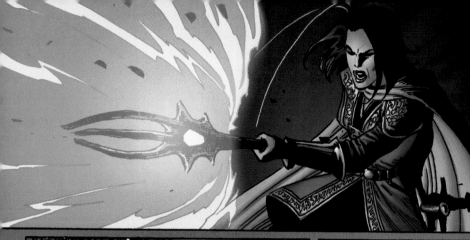

WHERE *ARE* YOU, CREATURE?

KRATCH

YAAAAH!

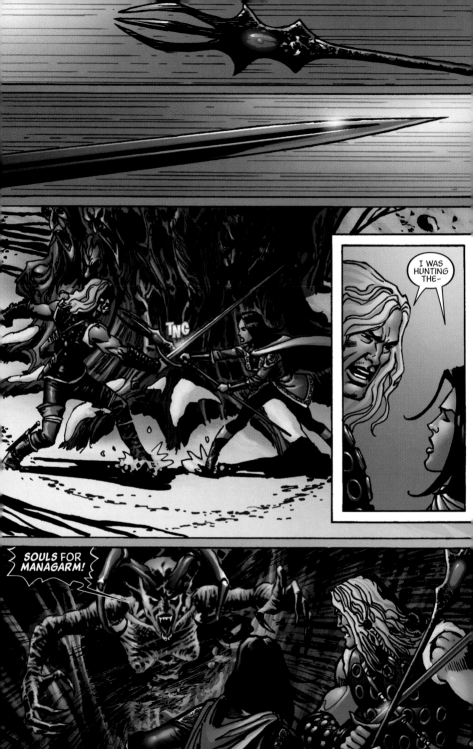

Eh?

FUCK

RUN, BARBARIAN.

NOW.

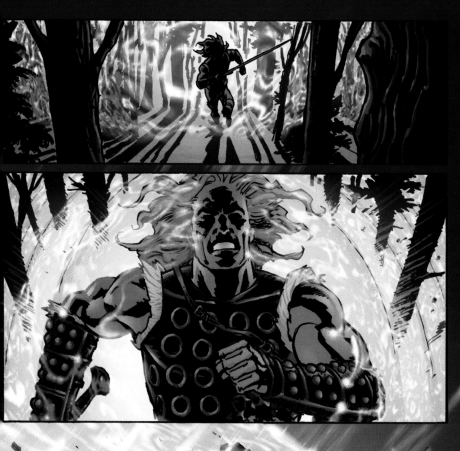

FMP

ONE STONE *STARTED* THE BLAZE.

ANOTHER IS ALREADY PUTTING IT *OUT.*

FWMP

I HAVE YET ANOTHER...TO *HEAL* YOUR WOUND?

YES.

YORF, MY FRIEND... YOU CAN'T HELP BEING ILL. IT COULD HAPPEN TO *ANY* OF US.

WE'VE BEEN HARD ON YOU. WE KNOW THAT, AND WE'RE *SORRY*.

YOU SHOULD LIE DOWN. GET SOME *REST*.

...OH, STOPPED MOVING, THANK ALL THE GODS...

REALLY?

INDEED. WE'RE MAKING VERY GOOD TIME.

AYE, AND IT'S THE LONG SLOW SIMMER THAT MAKES *VENGEANCE* WORTH IT IN THE END.

WELL...

...JUST FOR A MOMENT.

SNNNORRR

HEH.

HE'LL HAVE TO RUN ALL DAY.

AND *THEN* FACE THE WRATH OF MANAGARM.

...OH, YOU MOTHERLESS, GODS' CURSED SONS OF...

WAKEY-WAKEY...

...TIME TO PLAY.

YAH!

I WOULDN'T *MOVE* IF I WERE YOU. THIS *VINE* IS THE ONLY THING KEEPING YOU FROM BECOMING YORF THE *ONE-EYED*.

NOW, TELL ME ABOUT THE *GIRL*...

...AND I *PROMISE* I WON'T *CUT* THE VINE.

53

ALL RIGHT, ALL RIGHT, I'LL *TELL* YOU...

=SNIFF=

I'VE TOLD YOU EVERYTHING.

NOW SET ME FREE!

BUT THAT WASN'T THE DEAL. I SAID I WOULDN'T *CUT* THE VINE.

REALLY THERE'S NO NEED.

IT LOOKS *JUST* ABOUT READY TO GIVE ALL ON ITS OWN...

NO...

YIEERRHHHHHH

dip
dip
drip

SO, YOU TOOK THAT GIRL FOR *REVENGE*, NOW DID YOU?

WELL, *THAT'S* SOMETHING GRAVE MUNGO CAN UNDERSTAND...

HAHAHAHAHAHAHA

NEARLY SUNDOWN, MOIRA.

A FINE WAY TO SPEND YOUR DAY, WANDERING ABOUT WITH AN *UNBELIEVER*, IGNORING YOUR CHORES AT THE MISSION.

I'VE PUT IN AS GOOD A WORK DAY AS IT *GETS*, I THINK.

YOU'RE NOT LEFT WITH MUCH IN THE WAY OF *ANSWERS*, ARE YOU?

A *FIEND* LIKE THIS, REVEALING ITSELF ON THE MATERIAL PLANE?

I WASN'T LEFT WITH MUCH IN THE WAY OF *OPTIONS*.

FAIR ENOUGH.

BUT YOU'RE RIGHT. I HAVE QUESTIONS. DID SOMEONE *SUMMON* THIS ABOMINATION?

Ah... AND THERE IS THE MATTER OF *MANAGARM*, THE NAME SHE UTTERED.

I DON'T FOLLOW.

MANAGARM'S A DEMON. A *TRUE* DEMON. A LESSER FIEND WORSHIPPED BY THE GIANTS OF THIS LAND.

THEIR GOD OF WAR AND VENGEANCE.

THE *GIANTS*... POSSIBLE, I SUPPOSE.

STILL, IT IS CONVENIENT THAT THE FIEND ONLY **WOUNDED** ALPINADORANS CURIOUS ABOUT THE LIGHT FROM OUR MISSION...

...LEAVING THEM IN **MORTAL DANGER** IF THEY DIDN'T CONVERT AND GAIN OUR HEALING MAGICS.

AND IT HAD NO COMPUNCTION ABOUT **KILLING** THE ONLY ONES WHO SURVIVED THE NIGHT...

...THE ONES WHO SOUGHT TO GET AWAY AND WARN **OTHERS** WHO MIGHT COME THIS WAY.

YOU THINK SOMEONE AT YOUR **MISSION** SUMMONED THIS CREATURE?

I DON'T KNOW, IT'S JUST...

...ABBOT GREENE...

HE DOESN'T **CARE** ABOUT THE DELICATE BALANCE OF BELIEFS BETWEEN OUR PEOPLES, THE THINGS THAT CAN **DIVIDE** AND LEAD TO –

BY ALL THAT'S HOLY...

"...IT'S BEGUN!"

DEMON!

WHAT HAVE YOU DONE WITH MY *DAUGHTER?*

STOP!

YOU THINK I WOULD RISK THIS MISSION BY KIDNAPPING YOUR DAUGHTER?

THINK, CHIEFTAIN BYGGVIR. WHY WOULD I *DO* THAT?

TRYING TO *TRICK* ME, GREENE...

WE'VE SEEN **NO GIANTS**. WHAT ARE YOU–

YOUR MAGIC **CONTROLS** THEM, MONK...

...AND YOU USED THEM TO TAKE OUR CHIEFTAIN'S DAUGHTER!

WE DID **NOTHING** OF THE KIND! WE–

FOOLS...

ALL OF YOU! YOU **WILL** LISTEN TO ME...

...OR MY **FLAMES** WILL **BURN YOU** WHERE YOU STAND!

SISTER MOIRA...THINK **CAREFULLY** ABOUT THIS.

DEMON **WITCH**...

...I'M NOT LISTENING TO YOUR—

WHAP

DON'T BE AN *ASS*, BYGGVIR.

...OW...

MOIRA IS ACTUALLY VERY GOOD...

...AT *BURNING* THINGS.

I HAVE THE ORACLE GLASS AND THE GEMSTONES REQUIRED.

AWAKE, CREATURE. THE SLEEP OF DEATH IS TOO GOOD FOR YOU.

WELCOME BACK TO LIFE, DEMONESS...

...AND TO PAIN.

YOU SERVE MANAGARM, THE DEMON LORD OF VENGEANCE WORSHIPPED BY THE GIANTS.

AND IT WAS THE *GIANTS* WHO TOOK CHIEFTAIN BYGGVIR'S DAUGHTER, USING MAGIC NOT UNLIKE *YOURS*.

I BURN...

YOU *ATTACKED* THIS PLACE, CREATURE. WAS IT TO STOP THE ABELLICANS FROM HELPING BYGGVIR FIND HIS DAUGHTER?

TELL US WHAT YOU KNOW ABOUT THE *GIRL*....

I ADMIT, I WAS ANGRY AT FIRST, BUT YOU'VE BROUGHT ABOUT EXACTLY WHAT I WANTED: AN ALLIANCE WITH THE ALPINADORANS.

YOU *ARE* SPECIAL, MOIRA. AN APT PUPIL.

YOUR CONTROL OF MAGIC IS *STAGGERING*...

...LIKE YOUR *BEAUTY*.

WHAT OF THE ALPINADORANS WHO *DIED* AT OUR MISSION?

BYGGVIR AND HIS PEOPLE KNOW NOTHING OF IT. WE SHOULD KEEP IT THAT WAY.

WOULD YOU THREATEN THIS FRAGILE PEACE?

BUT–

BELIEVE ME, DEAR CHILD...

...THEY WILL FIND *NO* GRAVES.

MOIRA? WHERE ARE YOU GOING?

TO *HUNT* FOR DINNER...

"...SUDDENLY, I'M VERY **MUCH** IN THE MOOD TO KILL SOMETHING."

KRAKK

KRAAAAAK

AAH!

BY SAINT ABELLE...

...BUT SO AM I!

≥HACK≥

≥KOFF KOFF≥

YOU HAVE MY THANKS. IT'S NOT EVERY DAY ONE HAS TO DEAL WITH AN ORPHANED GUARDIAN OF THE GREAT OLD ONES.

MY NAME IS MOIRA, OF THE ABELLICAN FAITH.

GRAVE MUNGO, OF THE POWRIES OF BEN-SE-LA.

THEN ARE YOU *HUNGRY*, BY ANY CHANCE, GRAVE MUNGO?

HEH.

...SUPPOSE I SHOULDN'T MENTION I WAS REACHING FOR THE *STAFF*...

THEY'RE COMING... I CAN ALMOST *TASTE* THEIR MAN-FLESH...

AH. YOU'RE AWAKE. WELCOME TO THE FORTRESS OF MANAGARM, DAUGHTER OF MY ENEMY.

YOUR TRIAL BY FIRE BEGINS *NOW*.

SO WHAT BRINGS YOU HERE, GRAVE MUNGO?

AYE, FOR US, TOO.

IT'S ABOUT A GIRL.

...DIFFERENT, THOUGH, I'M SURE.

I'M SURE.

UM...DO YOU HAVE A *FAMILY* WAITING FOR YOU, SOME-WHERE? A PLACE YOU CALL HOME?

WORTHLESS TURD! LAYABOUT!

WITLESS FOOL, BUILDING USELESS TOYS...GET OUT THERE AND *PILLAGE* WITH THE REST OF THEM!

FATHER'S A TURD! FATHER'S A TURD!

MOTHER SAYS HE'S NOT EVEN OUR *REAL*—

NO.

NO ONE.

FAITHFUL WARRIORS, *TO ME!* I HAVE THE...

...WHAT?

LOOKING FOR *THIS,* LITTLE MAN? THE MAGIC GEMSTONES *YOU ALONE* CARRIED?

I FIND YOUR LACK OF TRUST IN YOUR FELLOW PRIESTS...

...REWARDING.

ATTACK!

SO TELL ME, GRAVE MUNGO, WHY ARE YOU DOING THIS?

SHUT UP. YOU'RE NOT EVEN *REAL,* ELENE.

BEEN OUT IN THIS DAMN COLD *TOO* LONG...

...SEEING THINGS NOW...

HUMOR ME. *MAYHAP* I'LL GO AWAY.

MY KIDNAPPERS ARE PREPARING TO *SACRIFICE* ME EVEN NOW. YOU CAN'T HOPE TO DEFEAT A *LEGION* OF *GIANTS* ON YOUR OWN.

...MORE WITH THE KILLING, LESS WITH THE TALKING. *THEN* WE'LL SEE...

ARE YOU IN *LOVE* WITH ME? DO YOU HONESTLY THINK I COULD LOVE *YOU,* TOO?

OR IS IT *GLORY* YOU SEEK? TO WEAR THE MANTLE OF A *HERO?*

A *FORTUNE?* A *FRESH START?*

GREAT *MOTHER* FROM THE *DEEP...*

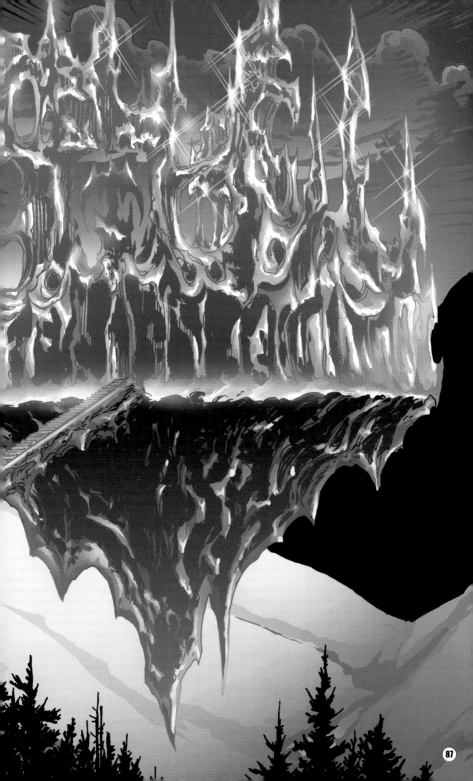

BUT...

...THAT *GAP* MUST BE *TEN FEET*, AT *LEAST!*

BY THE *TEETH* OF THE GREAT OLD ONES, HOW AM I SUPPOSED TO GET *ACROSS* THAT BLASTED THING?

HOW WOULD I KNOW?

I'M A PART OF *YOU*, GRAVE MUNGO. A VISION CONJURED BY YOUR WEARY AND SOMEWHAT *LIMITED* MIND.

BESIDES...

...YOU NEVER ANSWERED *MY* QUESTIONS.

SO EVEN IF I *COULD* TELL YOU HOW TO GET ACROSS...

...*WHY* WOULD I?

WAIT!

...DON'T GO...

SONS OF CURS! THIS IS ALL *YOUR* FAULT!

FILTHY, ROTTEN, MISBEGOTTEN LUMPS OF DUNG ON GIANT LEGS, WHEN I GET MY *HANDS* ON YOU CRETINS...

THE *EXCUSE*, YOU MEAN...

WHAT?

ALL THAT BLOOD, THEN OUR MANAGARM WILL RISE.

SHE'LL BE HACKED TO PIECES, I THINK. A THOUSAND CUTS.

OH, YES. IT WAS A THIRST FOR *REVENGE* THAT GAVE THAEL THE GUMPTION, IF YOU WOULD CALL IT THAT, TO FINALLY *RALLY* THE SCATTERED TRIBES.

BUT THIS DAY HAS BEEN *LONG* OVERDUE.

AT LEAST, SHE'LL BE CLEANED AND PRETTY FOR IT.

IN THE BEGINNING...

WHITE ROBE NOW.

BRIGHT RED, ONCE LORD THAEL GETS STARTED.

I'M TOLD YOU PASSED THE RUINS OF ONE OF OUR CITIES ON THE WAY HERE.

IT WAS *HUMANS*, LIKE YOUR FATHER, WHO LONG AGO DESTROYED OUR WAY OF LIFE. WHO MADE US INTO *ANIMALS*.

ONLY THE BLOOD OF ONE WHO HAS *WRONGED* US CAN SUMMON MANAGARM. YOUR *FATHER'S* BLOOD RUNS IN YOUR VEINS, CHILD...

THAT MAKES YOU *JUST* WHAT WE NEED.

AS TO THIR, THE ONE WHOSE *SKULL* YOUR FATHER HUNG LIKE A TROPHY ON HIS WALL, I KNEW HER.

HONESTLY, I COULDN'T CARE *LESS* THAT SHE'S DEAD...

...*BUT* FOR WHAT HER DEATH WILL BRING.

GEYSERS OF BLOOD. GEYSERS THAT MIGHT EVEN REACH US IN THE BACK.

BLOOD ON THE ICE. A SWEET DELICACY WHEN IT FREEZES.

A TREAT LATER, PERHAPS, FOR OUR DARLING BROTHER, THEOLLUS.

EVER TASTED MAN-FLESH?

WHEN SEASONED JUST RIGHT IT TASTES LIKE—

MODGUD COMES. AWAY, AWAY!

ONCE YOUR BLOOD IS SPILLED, MANAGARM WILL SET FIRE TO THE WORLD OF HUMANS. AND *WE* SHALL BE SPARED... TO SERVE HIM.

TO FEED HIM... HEH... OUR VERY *SOULS*, IF NEED BE.

THEN YOU REMAIN *CATTLE*.

WE ARE HIS *DEVOTED!*

SLAP

BUT IN THE END... PERHAPS.

AYE, PERHAPS IT'S WHAT WE *ALL* ARE, WILLINGLY OR NO.

SOULS FOR MANAGARM, MY LITTLE DOVE...

"...SOULS FOR MANAGARM."

THIS PLACE...

...WHERE...?

COME NOW, ANDACANAVAR, YOU SPENT HALF YOUR LIFE HERE.

SURELY YOU RECOGNIZE *ANDUR'BLOUGH ININNINESS*, THE VALLEY OF MIST AND THE *TOUEL'ALFAR*, THE ELVES WHO TRAINED YOU.

IMPOSSIBLE.

I WAS IN ALPINADOR WITH MOIRA, THE ABELLICANS, AND BYGGVIR'S PEOPLE.

WE WERE SEARCHING FOR—

WE KNOW *VERY WELL* WHAT YOU SEEK, YOUNG RANGER. IT IS THAT WHICH YOU HAVE SOUGHT SINCE YOU WERE A *CHILD*.

BUT KNOW THIS.

THE LINK BETWEEN THE REAL AND THE *UNREAL* WORLD MAY—OR MAY NOT—BE *STRONGER* THAN THE ONE YOU SEEK TO FORGE BETWEEN YOUR PEOPLE AND THE OUTSIDERS...

"...BREAK ONE, FORGE ANOTHER. IT IS YOUR *DESTINY*. IT'S..."

...Ugh... WHA...?

ALL *YOUR* FAULT GREENE.

MY FAULT? HOW CAN ANY OF THIS POSSIBLY BE MY FAULT?

THESE CREATURES KNEW THEIR PLACE UNTIL YOU LOT CAME ALONG.

YOUR DEMON MAGIC *EMPOWERED* THEM SOMEHOW.

BY ALL THAT'S HOLY, BYGGVIR, FREE ME FROM THESE CHAINS AND I'LL *SHOW* YOU WHAT I CAN DO WITHOUT A *BIT* OF MAGIC!

HOW LONG HAVE THEY BEEN AT IT?

...AS LONG AS I'VE BEEN AWAKE.

SO THEY BROUGHT US TO THE FORTRESS OF MANAGARM? THE *EXACT* PLACE WE WERE SEEKING?

AYE, *FUNNY* THAT.

ESPECIALLY CONSIDERING WE'RE PRISONERS, WEAPONLESS, AND AT THE MERCY OF KILLERS.

SAVED US A LOT OF... ⇒NGH⇐ ...WALKING AND RIDING.

GOOD A REASON AS I CAN SEE FOR BEING AMBUSHED AND SLAUGHTERED NEAR TO A MAN.

I CAN THINK OF WORSE COMPANIONS TO SPEND MY DYING MOMENTS WITH, MOIRA.

Ah...

FILTHY WRETCH!

MUST I REMIND YOU THAT YOUR *DAUGHTER* IS SOMEWHERE IN THIS KEEP?

...ELENE...?

MY DAUGHTER!

HOW *DARE* YOU SPEAK OF HER?

YOUR DAUGHTER. YOUR POSSESSION. YOUR *CHATTEL.*

DO YOU EVEN KNOW THE FIRST THING ABOUT HER?

HER DREAMS? HER ASPIRATIONS?

...ABBOT, WHAT ARE YOU DOING...?

SOMEHOW, I DOUBT THAT YOU DO. *HOURS* WE'VE BEEN HERE AND NOT *ONCE* HAVE YOU—

I'LL DECIDE WHEN WE SPEAK OF HER! I'LL DECIDE ALL THERE IS TO *BE* DECIDED ABOUT HER!

NO ONE TAKES FROM ME WHAT IS *MINE.*

NO ONE!

A UNION OF MY PEOPLE AND OUTSIDERS. I MUST HAVE BEEN MAD.

SO THEN, ARE YOU CERTAIN WE ARE ALL WHO SURVIVED?

I'VE HEARD VOICES. I THINK THERE MAY BE A FEW MORE IN ANOTHER CELL.

MY PEOPLE?

OR YOURS?

FORGIVE ME, MOIRA. WITH MY DOUBTS, I DISHONOR YOUR FRIENDSHIP, FREELY GIVEN.

AND I DISHONOR THOSE WHO RAISED ME, GAVE ME A PURPOSE, HOPE AND DREAMS...

WITHOUT DREAMS, WE ARE AS ONE DEAD. THAT IS WHAT THE TOUEL'ALFAR TAUGHT ME WHEN I WAS BUT A CHILD.

I HAVE TURNED MY BACK ON SO MUCH THAT WAS CLEAR TO ME.

WHAT'S CLEAR TO ME RIGHT NOW IS THAT WHAT I WANT IS MY FREEDOM...

...AND THE HEADS OF A FEW GIANTS ON STICKS.

BEST OF ALL, I THINK I KNOW HOW TO GET BOTH. A VERY GOOD THING INDEED...

"...BECAUSE WE CAN'T EXPECT *ANYONE* TO COME AND SAVE US."

AROOOo

WOLVES!

GATHER THE *YOUNG!* RETURN TO THE FORTRESS!

THEY HUNT IN PACKS!

MY COUSIN, GENDRETH, BIG AS HE WAS, WAS OUT HUNTING AND WAS BROUGHT DOWN AND *EATEN* BY A PACK.

PRAISE MANAGARM FOR THE *SAFETY* HIS KEEP PROVIDES.

I DON'T **SEE** ANY WOLVES. USUALLY THEY GATHER AT THE BASE OF THE BROKEN BRIDGE.

THEIR HOWLS HAVE STOPPED. STRANGE TO HAVE HEARD THEM AND NOT SEEN THEM.

LITTLE THEOLLUS HAS BEEN SO BRAVE. HE HASN'T CRIED **ONCE**. HE...

AROOO

WOOF.

Gah?

GUHHH...

BUT...

...A FRIEND GAVE THE GEM TO ME. HE NEVER SAID IT WAS–

YOU'VE BEEN WEARING AN AMETHYST GEMSTONE **BRIMMING** WITH MAGIC.

ITS VIBRATIONS ARE POWERFUL ENOUGH TO SET US FREE.

MORE DEMON MAGIC! RANGER, YOU'LL BE THE DEATH OF US ALL.

ON THE CONTRARY, HE'S THE ONLY ONE AMONG YOUR **THICKHEADED** KIND WHO UNDERSTANDS THAT MAGIC IS NOT EVIL.

HE MIGHT EVEN BE YOUR **SALVATION** ONE DAY.

FILTHY, TAINTED, SCUMLICKING–

HOLD STILL WHILE I–

NO!

I'LL STAY HERE AND *ROT* BEFORE I LET YOUR DEMON MAGICS *STEAL* MY *SOUL.*

FAMILIAR WORDS...

ABBOT GREENE...CHIEFTAIN BYGGVIR...YOUR PEOPLE ARE *DEAD.*

BUT ELENE *IS* ALIVE.

MY DAUGHTER?

HOW CAN YOU *KNOW* THAT?

BECAUSE OUR *HEADS* ARE STILL ATTACHED.

ALL RIGHT THEN, DAMN YOU...

"...FREE ME."

THEY WANT US TO WITNESS WHAT THEY HAVE PLANNED.

I WOULD SAY SO.

HOLD. THOSE VOICES, I HEAR THEM *AGAIN.* I—

SISTER MOIRA, THE *GEMSTONES* THE GIANTS TOOK FROM ME...THEY MUST BE HERE.

DO YOU UNDERSTAND WHAT I'M TELLING YOU?

ABBOT GREENE, I HAVE THE RANGER'S AMETHYST, I COULD...

RANGER, *TOUCH* MY DAUGHTER AND MY SPIRIT WILL RETURN TO *CRUSH* YOUR DAMN SKULL.

LIVE, CHILD, AND TELL ALL OF THIS DAY, WHEN ABELLICAN AND ALPINADORAN FOUGHT SIDE-BY-SIDE.

GO NOW!

TIME FOR THAEL, *KING* OF THE GIANTS, TO TASTE SWEET VENGEANCE!

YAAGH!

I... ...I THOUGHT...

ONE CUT AND YOUR BLOOD FEEDS THE FLAMES...

...AND *CALLS* TO MANAGARM.

I'LL SEE YOU DEAD FOR THIS.

NAY, CHILD. I AM DEAD INSIDE ALREADY.

NOTHING THAT HAPPENS TO ME AT THIS MOMENT TRULY MATTERS...

...BUT *YOU*...

...YOU ARE THE **HERALD**, THE BRINGER OF JUSTICE TO ME AND MY KIND.

FLESH OF HE WHO **WRONGED** ME.

CHILD OF THE **MONSTER** WHO TOOK MY WIFE AND CHILD FROM ME.

NO, I...

...WHAT'S HAPPENING...

YOU ARE THE AVATAR, DAUGHTER OF DESTRUCTION.

BY THE GODS, NO...

TELL US WHAT WE WANT TO KNOW...

...AND YOU **WON'T** DIE SCREAMING.

MUCH.

YOU'RE... RUNNING OUT OF TIME.

OUR LORD... OUR **GOD**... MANAGARM... HAS RISEN.

I CAN... **FEEL**... MANAGARM'S PRESENCE...IN THIS...FORTRESS. HIS **HOME.**

MAYHAP THAT'S TRUE. BUT HE'S

NOT

HERE

NOW.

I WOULD **TALK** NOW, IF I WERE YOU. SHE **WILL** CRUSH YOU TO DEATH AGAINST THAT WALL.

SLOWLY.

I'VE SEEN HER DO **FAR** WORSE.

PARDON ME...

...IT SEEMS *GRAVE MUNGO* IS ONE STEP AHEAD OF YOU LOT.

LOOKING FOR YOUR *WEAPONS*, I TAKE IT?

MY THANKS.

SO WHAT'S TO BE DONE WITH YOUR NEW FRIEND HERE?

I MEAN, YOU *CAN'T* VERY WELL LEAVE HIM ALIVE, NOW CAN YOU?

MANAGARM... *WILL...AVENGE...* ME...

ALL OF HUMANITY... WILL BURN... BEFORE HIS-

110

FWUMP

NEED HELP WITH THAT?

I CAN MANAGE.

≫HUFF≪
≫HUFF≪

...*THAT* WAS FOR MY *CAP*...

WHERE DID YOU FIND ALL THIS?

AH. LET'S SEE. WELL, IT *IS* TREASURE.

I'D TAKE A WILD GUESS AND SAY THE *TREASURE ROOM?*

WE'VE NEVER BEEN *FORMALLY* INTRODUCED.

I'M *ANDACANAVAR,* THE RANGER. THIS IS MOIRA, OF THE—

SHE AND I HAVE *MET.*

GRAVE, WHEN YOU WERE IN THAT ROOM, DID YOU SEE A SMALL BAG FILLED WITH *GEMSTONES* LIKE THIS?

NO. BUT I WASN'T *LOOKING* FOR IT, EITHER. IT'S SOME DISTANCE, BUT I COULD TAKE YOU THERE—

NO.
THE GIANT SAID MANAGARM HAS RISEN.

WE WERE BEING KEPT ALIVE TO *WITNESS* SOMETHING TO DO WITH ELENE, CHIEFTAIN BYGGVIR'S DAUGHTER...

"...WHICH MEANS **SHE'S** STILL ALIVE."

"WE HAVE TO FIND HER."

"AND **KILL** THIS DEMON MANAGARM BEFORE HE CAN SUMMON AN ARMY OF **FAR MORE** THAN JUST GIANTS TO THIS PLACE."

ONE OF MY FOLLOWERS IS **DEAD**.

IT IS THE **HUMANS**.

THEY **DARE** THIS AFFRONT **HERE**, IN THE **SANCTUARY** I HAVE PROVIDED FOR THE **GREAT CLANS**.

...AND I'LL **FINISH** THIS FIGHT ONCE AND FOR ALL.

PRETTY **ROCK.**

ME WANT.

NO, ME!

KEEP YOUR DEMON MAGIC **AWAY** FROM ME, GREENE!

I'LL **DIE** BEFORE LETTING YOU HEAL ME WITH THAT THING!

THE **HEMATITE** CAN DO MORE THAN HEAL...

...IT CAN ALSO SET THE SOUL **FREE** TO SEE THROUGH THE EYES OF OTHERS...

...AND TAKE **CONTROL** OF THEM.

COME **HERE**, CREATURE...

BY THE **WILL** OF **DANE THORSSON!**

→HRK←

SUCH **SAVAGERY**...

MAYHAP I'VE MISJUDGED YOU, GREENE.

WE'LL...TALK OF IT ANOTHER TIME. **NOW** WE MUST FIND YOUR DAUGHTER...

"...AND THE OTHERS."

THE POWRIE FIGHTS WELL.

IT'S THAT OR *DIE*. HARD FOR ME TO BE IMPRESSED.

TRY AND SEPARATE *ME* FROM MY TREASURE, EH?

COME, WRETCHED MONSTERS!

TASTE THE COLD **STEEL** OF GRAVE MUNGO'S AXE!

THEY JUST **KEEP** COMING!

AYE, IT'S LIKE THERE'S AN ENDLESS SUPPLY OF THEM.

NO, NOT ENDLESS...

...THOUGH ONE DAY, WHEN *YOUR KIND* IS DUST, THEIR NUMBERS WILL BE AS YOURS...

AND THIS WORLD WILL BE *THEIRS* TO RULE...

...FOR ME.

THAT'S BYGGVIR'S DAUGHTER!

...ELENE...

MANAGARM, YOU FILTHY, SCURRYING *ANIMALS.*

WHERE IS THIS VESSEL'S *SIRE?*

HERE, CHILD.

MY CHILD... A DEMON?

MY SOUL TO *YOURS*, CREATURE...

AGGGHHH!

MANAGARM IS *FALLEN!*

RUN!

NO, YOU FOOLS!

ELENE... I TOUCHED THEIR MINDS...

THEIR? WHAT DO YOU MEAN?

ELENE IS *ALIVE.*

THERE IS A TASK SHE MUST PERFORM, A CHOICE **SHE** MUST MAKE...

...TO **CONSECRATE** THIS UNION.

UNTIL THAT HAPPENS, THE **LINK** BINDING HER TO **MANAGARM** CAN BE BROKEN...

...AND THE **MEANS** TO DO SO ARE IN THIS **KEEP.**

THE TOUEL'ALFAR... IN MY DREAM, THEY TRIED TO TELL ME.

"THE LINK BETWEEN THE REAL AND THE UNREAL WORLDS..."

MOIRA, THIS WILL REQUIRE US **BOTH.** WHEN MY MIND TOUCHED ELENE'S...

...AND THAT OF THAT **THING...**

...I SAW THE HIDING PLACE OF THE BAG OF **GEMSTONES** THEY TOOK FROM ME.

WITH THEM, WE MIGHT–

YOU MIGHT **KILL** THIS THING AND **LEVEL** THIS GODS' CURSED PLACE.

ANDACANAVAR...

I'LL BE HERE...

...I WILL **ALWAYS** BE HERE FOR YOU.

LITTLE MEN...

WHAT **FUN** DO YOU HAVE IN STORE FOR ME THIS TIME, **LITTLE MEN?**

RELEASE HER, **DEMON!**

AH... YOUR SWORD IS ELVEN-FORGED SILVEREL.

IT **STINGS.**

Heh.

THIS VESSEL...

...I...

...DESIRED YOU. JOIN WITH ME AND I WILL BE...

...**GENEROUS.**

SHUT YOUR FILTHY **MOUTH** AND STAY AWAY FROM HIM. YOU ARE **MY** DAUGHTER!

YOU WILL **DO** AS I **SAY!**

ALL MY LIFE, YOU'VE TREATED ME AS YOUR **CHATTEL,** A SLAVE.

MANAGARM OFFERS ME POWER. **FREEDOM,** AND ALL I MUST DO TO JOIN WITH HIM **FOREVER** IS TAKE YOUR LIFE...

"...AND I CAN THINK OF *NO REASON* TO SPARE YOU..."

THE GEMSTONES... ARE *HERE?*

IN THIS FORTRESS, SOMEWHERE, YES...

I THINK YOU *SHOULD* KILL HIM.

IN *THIS* SPOT, MANAGARM WAS SUMMONED BY AN ACT OF *VENGEANCE.* A GESTURE OF ABSOLUTE DARKNESS.

ONLY AN EQUALLY POWERFUL GESTURE OF ITS OPPOSITE, *FORGIVENESS,* CAN SEVER ITS LINK TO THIS WORLD.

WHAT?

IF HE'S AS BAD AS ALL THAT, *DO IT.* BUT KILL HIM FOR *YOURSELF.* NOT BECAUSE THAT *THING* COMMANDS YOU.

FOR ALL OUR SAKES, I PRAY *YOU* CAN MAKE THAT GESTURE AND FORGIVE ME...

WHAT ARE YOU TALKING—

AGH!

...ON THE WAY DOWN.

TAKE MANAGARM'S POWER. DON'T LET A *DEMON* TAKE YOURS.

OTHERWISE, YOU'LL JUST BE A THRALL EX-CHANGING *ONE* MASTER FOR *ANOTHER*.

DAMN YOU, CHILD! I AM YOUR *FATHER!*

NO MORE.

RRUMBLE

NO!

IT'S...

...IT'S GONE. MANAGARM IS—

AYE, ELENE, AND THE PLACE IS FALLING *APART* AS A RESULT.

BYGGVIR! A LITTLE HELP, HERE!

DO AS YOU WILL WITH *HER*. IT'S NO CONCERN OF—

BYGGVIR!

YOU TOOK *EVERYTHING* FROM ME! YOU SLEW MY WIFE AND CHILD LIKE *ANIMALS!*

I'D *KILL* THEM *AGAIN!*

WE'LL FACE THIS—

LEAVE ME, DEMON. *THIS* IS WHAT I WANT.

FATHER...

THIS FORTRESS IS PERCHED OVER A CAVERN. MAGIC ALONE KEPT IT FROM FALLING.

WE MUST GET AWAY FROM HERE.

YOU TAKE ELENE. I'M NOT LEAVING WITHOUT—

NO...

SHE DIED WELL, RANGER...

...SHE DIED TO SAVE US ALL...

"...DON'T LET HER SACRIFICE BE FOR *NOTHING.*"

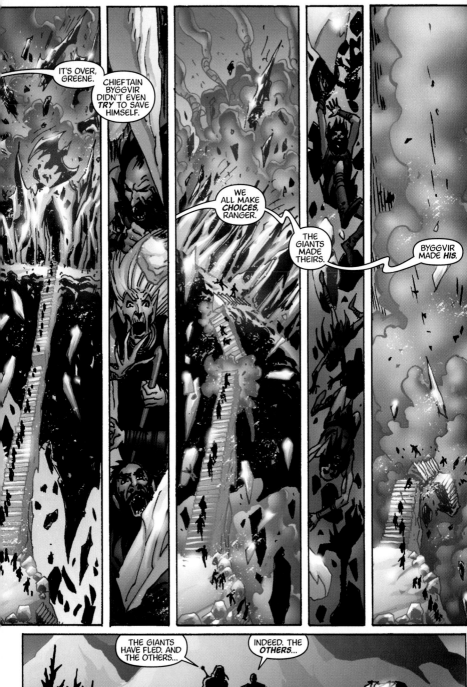

I TRIED TO TALK ELENE, YOUR FELLOW *ALPINADORAN*, OUT OF IT.

BUT YOU SAW FOR YOURSELF, SHE HAD *NO INTENTION* OF RETURNING HOME.

I HAD HOPED FOR THE *UNION* BETWEEN MY FAITH AND YOUR PEOPLE, LED BY HER, AND PERHAPS *ONE DAY*—

MOIRA.

YES.

MOIRA. HER BODY *CANNOT* BE RETRIEVED. IT IS LOST...

"...WITH SO MANY OTHER THINGS."

WHERE DO WE GO?

SOMEPLACE, WARM, I THINK. THERE ARE LANDS WHERE PEOPLE KNOW *NOTHING* OF MY KIND.

AND I WISH TO BE AS FAR FROM HERE AS POSSIBLE.

AGREED.

BUT HOW WILL WE LIVE? I KNOW *LITTLE* OF OTHER LANDS, BUT I'VE READ THAT MOST ARE HOSTILE TO OUTSIDERS.

CLINK

THE ABELLICAN *GEMSTONES...*

HOW WILL WE LIVE? WITH A TREASURE LIKE *THIS* IN OUR POCKETS?

QUITE WELL, I WOULD IMAGINE.

HA HA HA HA

The End

TIMELINE

600

God's Year 621 — The gemstones fall from the heavens

770

God's Year 769 — Andacanavar is born

780

God's Year 777 — Andacanavar begins training with the elves

790

God's Year 790 — Andacanavar returns to his people as a Ranger

TRIAL BY FIRE *(Mini-series One)*
God's Year 792 — Andacanavar is 23

800

THE DEMON AWAKENS *(Book One)*
God's Year 816 — The Demon Dactyl rises and Avelyn Desbris enters
the Abellican Order

820

God's Year 821 — The gemstones fall from the heavens

God's Year 825 — The Demon Dactyl is presumed destroyed with Mt. Aida

THE DEMON SPIRIT *(Book Two)*
God's Year 825 — The battle against the Demon Dactyl is rejoined

THE DEMON APOSTLE *(Book Three)*
God's Years, late 825 to 826 — The Demon Dactyl is destroyed at tragic cost
(Andacanavar is involved in the conflict)

MORTALIS *(Book Four)*
God's Years 827 to 834 — The Rosy Plague *(during which Andacanavar
convinces his people to fight beside the forces of Honce-the-Bear and to
accept the healing magic of the Hand of Avelyn)*

830

840

ASCENDANCE *(Book Five)* & *TRANSCENDANCE (Book Six)*
God's Year 840 — Jilseponie becomes Queen and her wedding is attended
by 71-year-old Andacanavar

IMMORTALIS *(Book Seven)* **God's Years 841 to 8XX** — The
kingdoms of Behren and Honce-the-Bear go to war, and Jilseponie confronts
her son, King Aydrian Boudabras

GLOSSARY

Abellicans — The spiritual followers of Saint Abelle. Members of an austere religious order that gather the magical gemstones that fall from the sky every 200 years and wield their power. Despite their monk-like robes and seemingly passive demeanor, Abellicans are trained for combat and conditioned to endure harsh physical rigors.

Abellican Order — The order's public face is benevolent, but in its highest ranks the order is rife with ambition, corruption, and murder. The vast majority of their followers are unaware of the faith's darker side. The Abellican Order holds great power in the kingdom of Honce-the-Bear.

Alpinadorans — A fierce Norse-like people rooted in tradition and suspicious of all those outside Alpinador's borders. The hard and brutal Alpinadorans, who resemble Vikings, worship a pantheon of gods and believe all magic is evil. They live in the frozen inhospitable lands north of Honce-the-Bear.

Andur'Blough Inninness — Also known as the Valley of Mist. Home of the mysterious and secretive Touel'alfar (elves), located in the mountains west of the Wilderlands. The mists enshrouding the valley are magical in nature and maintained to keep away the curious.

Corona — A world besieged by demonwars. The setting for our tales.

Frost Giants — A once proud, accomplished race whose civilization has been destroyed by Alpinadorans. Driven into the mountains of Alpinador, they have been on the verge of extinction due to lack of food and shelter. Their worship of the demon Managarm has put these angry people into a position of power to seek vengeance against humanity. Also known as fomorians.

Gemstone Magic — This form of magic comes from stones that fall onto one island on Corona every 200 years. Each gemstone has a different power. For example, hematite can heal, while rubies create fire, and graphite sends lightning bolts.

Managarm — A true lesser fiend, Managarm is the demon lord of war and vengeance worshipped by the Frost Giants. He is represented by a wolf-like symbol because the wolves are the one predator the giants fear and respect. Managarm and his followers command dark earth elemental magic.

Powries — The red-capped dwarfs of the Weathered Isles. Traditionally, they are known to serve only their own selfish interests. Using barrel boats, they attack other ships in the Mirianic Ocean. The powries are great fighters. By dipping their red caps in the blood of their victims, they gain enhanced strength and fortitude.

Rangers — Humans trained by the elves to protect the many lands of Corona, inform the elves of problems, and ensure justice for innocents. They are usually selected by elves as children and trained for eight to ten years.

Touel'alfar — The elves. They stand approximately three feet tall, and they are slender with golden-hued skin and wings that can be used to fly short distances. The elves usually remain apart from the rest of the world except in their practice of recruiting and training human Rangers. Their magic is natural and comes from all things good in nature. They are excellent craftspeople and use silverel to make bows and swords for the rangers.

Weathered Isles — The home of the powries. A group of stony islands where no crops can grow, forcing the powries to act as pirates and raiders for their needs. This is where Grave's home, Ben-Se-La, is located.

Three Ships

BY R.A. SALVATORE

Illustrations by Butch Guice,
Mark Pennington and Laura Martin

I t stank.

The smell of sweat hung thick in the humid air of the cramped quarters, where forty dwarves sat two across on small benches, their short and strong legs pedaling tirelessly through the hours. Up in front of the twin lines, Besk Morkis called out the cadence, punctuating his count every so often with a threat or an insult. He wasn't speaking in the tongue common to the powries of the Weathered Isles, but rather, in the strange and singsong Behrenese language. Ever since this crew had put out from the north, Besk, the old veteran who had traveled in the southern waters extensively over the years, had been using Behrenese almost exclusively. Besk was a tall one as the dwarves, the powries, went, standing a full five feet, and two inches above that if one counted his bright red beret — the bloodiest and brightest beret of all the forty-one, which was why Besk was the commander, after all.

Back near the middle of the barrel boat, Grave Mungo, the youngest and least experienced of the crew, hardly listened to the nasty coxswain, having long ago fallen into the pedaling rhythm. He ignored the complaints and ignored the heat (and how much hotter it had become since the barrelboat had left the northern waters of the Mirianic!), and ignored the continuing burn in his legs from muscles too long at their work. Unlike the great sailing ships of the humans, the powries had fashioned craft that did not depend on the wind. The mostly-submerged barrelboat was moved by a propeller, turned by the sweat and strength of the dwarven crew.

No matter how hard he tried, Grave could not ignore the stench. They had plowed through a storm the night before, the swells tipping the barrelboat all about, and more than a few had vomited.

Besk had promised them that they could stop that night, once they'd put the storm far behind them, and clean the boat up a bit, perhaps even getting out on the deck in turns.

But only if they worked hard through all the day, of course, and so the cadence was particularly swift now, with vicious Besk determined to make up for time lost in the gale.

"Put yer back into it, ye durned dogs!" he shouted at one point, and he stormed down the center aisle past a few benches and punched one powrie hard in the shoulder. "Bah, ye start pulling harder or I'm giving ye to the sharks!"

It was no idle threat, they all knew, for Besk had done just that to another of the crew soon after they had put out from the coastal village of Ben-se-la back in their homeland of the Weathered Isles. Of course, there were no sharks in that northern, cold water, but the powrie had died all the same, his limbs going numb, and then his face turned all frosty about the beard. With a look of puzzlement, the doomed dwarf slowly slipped beneath the dark and cold water.

Grave knew that Besk had done that just for effect, and that the doomed powrie had been chosen and condemned before the barrelboat had ever left the docks. Likely the poor dwarf had committed some minor crime against one of

the town bosses, and so Besk had paid good coin for the privilege of killing him. It was all done, of course, to show the others on the crew that Besk would tolerate nothing from them. At least, that was the supposed point of it all, but given the typical existence of the powries, it seemed to Grave that the torture of the doomed dwarf was redundant to the point of ineffectiveness.

More likely, he realized, Besk had done it just for the pleasure of killing.

Grave couldn't blame him.

Aveela Ashkar stood at the prow of the swift *Baubler*, feeling the wind and the spray on her dark-skinned face. Every so often, the woman shook out her long black hair, a mane so black that it held its luster against the continual barrage of sea salt. Neither did her dark brown eyes lose their twinkling edge. How she loved the wind and the spray, and the thrill of the hunt.

In these more northern waters, where the swells were higher and the storms more fierce, *Baubler* did seem a bit unbalanced and out of place. She was a two-masted jumper, a design of ship peculiar to southern Behren that was somewhat a cross between a schooner and a catamaran, and as such, she didn't cut deep into the Mirianic waters, but rather glided across them as if skating on ice. She was further north than her normal hunting grounds, a fact that made Aveela and the rest of *Baubler*'s crew uneasy. For she was not a heavily-armored craft, and possessed only a single catapult, and not a large one. Her skill lay in maneuverability, and in the archery and sword fighting talents of the crack crew.

In the south, *Baubler* would simply run from the heavier ships commissioned by the ruling yatol priests. Though some of those ships were actually faster, particularly in a strong wind, they'd have no chance of catching her in those shoal-filled southern coastal waters. While *Baubler* could skim over the sharp edges of submerged reefs, the yatols' ships could not, and in her thirteen years aboard, Aveela had watched more than one pursuing caravel or schooner break apart on the unforgiving coral.

Up here, though, the waters were deep, and *Baubler* could be vulnerable.

Aveela and all the others knew that, but when Prattle Moojees had informed the crew that they were heading to the waters off the coast of Jacintha, in northern Behren, not a one dared question him.

Prattle didn't take well to being questioned.

"You catch a flash of blue, little one?" came a throaty baritone voice behind Aveela, and the reference to her as "little one" was even more of an identifier than Prattle's guttural tones.

"Not a fleck of light in all the waters," Aveela answered, and she turned to regard the huge man as he walked up beside her and grasped his leathery hands — paws big enough to cover her entire face! — about the rail.

Even though she was no longer a child, Aveela felt like one, comfortably so, when she was standing next to the giant pirate. He stood at least a foot taller than her five-and-a-half foot frame, and was twice her girth. Aveela had never seen a man eat as much as the gluttonous Prattle; the crew of *Baubler* even joked that they needed three storerooms on the ship, one for the booty, one for their supplies, and one for Prattle's food. The man always smelled of cooking grease, and his beard always seemed thick with the stuff, and when he smiled, which was often, an observant person could tell just about everything he had eaten over the last few days.

Aveela looked past all those unpleasantries when she considered Prattle, though. Her father had been one of his loyal crew, out of Cosinnida in the south, for many years, and when the man had been killed on the high seas, Prattle hadn't hesitated to fill his role with young Aveela.

So it was with most of *Baubler*'s crew. Cutthroats all, as vicious a pirate crew sailing the Behren coast, they were family. Aveela would leap in front of Prattle and take a spear aimed for his heart, and she knew that he would do no less for her.

"I can see what you're thinking, little one," Prattle said suddenly, and he gave a toothy grin. "You're not much for liking my choices here, are you?"

For a moment, Aveela bit back her retort, but then reconsidered and decided that if she was to question Prattle, this would be the time, perhaps the only time. "Bloody caps?" she asked.

"You've cut us a partnership with the nasty little dwarves of the northern seas?"

Prattle sighed as he looked out over the rail. "Aye," he admitted. "And it weren't an easy choice. Nasty little things, them powries."

"I heard that they dip their hats in the blood of their victims, then put them back atop their hairy heads."

"True enough," said Prattle. "Berets. And the more blood the caps soak in, the brighter they shine. I think there's magic about them even beyond their color, though I can't be sure."

"I do not believe that I am going to like our partners much."

"What's to lose?" asked Prattle. "If you've killed your enemy anyway, then what's the harm of taking a bit of his spilling blood?"

"They are not like us," Aveela argued.

"No, not a bit. And that's the beauty, can't you see? The merchants we come upon will have no answers to a powrie barrelboat. By Chezru, they won't even know the damned thing's there until it's too late!"

"*Baubler*'s never needed any help in catching and killing a merchant ship."

"But there's nothing to lose," said Prattle. "The powries want only enough food to keep them moving along the hunt. Booty's all ours, little one."

"Then why are they doing it?" Aveela asked. She turned to face Prattle directly, and stared at him hard until he looked from the open waters to her. "Why?"

Prattle gave a helpless laugh. "For the fun."

Aveela looked back out to the open waters.

"Just think of them as an extension of *Baubler*," Prattle advised. "An underwater ram attached to our own ship, and with no adds to the crew."

Aveela nodded, and the huge pirate laughed and slapped her on the back, then started away.

It wasn't quite so easy for Aveela to dismiss her uneasiness over all of this, however. They were in unfamiliar waters now, too far north to make a run for the safety of the reefs, and with Jacintha garrison warships in the area. Even the merchants they would likely encounter up here would be larger and more heavily armed than those sailing the shallower waters off the Cossinida coast.

And the powries! An extension of *Baubler*? An ally who wanted nothing in return? Perhaps it was true, Aveela logically understood, but she couldn't shake the unsettling echo of Prattle's explanation of their motivations.

For the fun.

Aveela had just started to shake her head when a blue flash far out to the northeast caught her eye. The powrie signal.

Prattle's nasty little friends had arrived.

Grave Mungo climbed the short ladder into the hatchway of the barrelboat and slid open the small window for forward viewing. Designed and weighted to float just along the surface, the majority of a powrie barrelboat was always below the water, with just a bit of curving deck and the small hatch tower peeking up above the waves.

For a long while, Grave watched the methodical breaking of the water about the forward deck as the craft cut through the water. Up ahead, he saw the sails of *Baubler*, leading them in the hunt. How much easier and more comfortable that method of water travel seemed to Grave. He wished that he could be up there, feeling the wind and the spray instead of in here, in the heat and stench and stagnant air.

The powrie glanced down the ladder and all about, his face flushed as if he feared that even thinking such thoughts might evoke the wrath of Besk Morkis. The last thing he wanted was to be put right back on the pedaling line; every dwarf aboard relished his time in the tower.

Distracted by his daydreams, Grave at first didn't even notice the white sails of a second ship coming into view, ahead and off to starboard.

Baubler veered to intercept, her tall masts bending low, and Grave could see her crew scrambling, readying weapons and rushing to their battle positions. For a long moment, Grave just watched it all, enchanted by the deadly dance. He saw the second ship cut even lower in a sudden and desperate turn, saw *Baubler*'s catapult send a spinning missile of jagged chains out high and far.

Finally the powrie hooked his feet on the ladder and slid down to drop

between his pedaling companions. "They got one on the run!" he called to Besk, who turned eagerly. "Running off to starboard!"

Grave ran to take his seat at the pedals, then, while Besk made for the tower and began calling out instructions. "Seven to four!" he shouted before he even climbed up to regard the hunt, his numbers indicating that three of every seven dwarves on the starboard should cease their pedaling so that the unbalanced propeller spins would quickly begin to realign the ship.

Once he got up in the tower, Besk altered his commands continually, maneuvering the lumbering boat.

Circling for the kill.

Bow in hand, Aveela took her place among the line of archers. Methodically, the crack crew of *Baubler* went about their work, deck hands running pots of burning pitch into position along the archer line, catapult crew fast reloading and letting another cluster of spinning chains off into the clear sky, tenders fast dropping the ship's vulnerable canvas to battle sail.

"We've got her mainsail torn!" the lookout shouted down.

Aveela nodded and smiled. This was her favorite part. The hunt, the thrilling pursuit, the tense moments before battle was joined.

Baubler glided in as the prey, a short and stout two-masted caravel, dropped her sails and slowly turned a broadside to the smaller craft.

Prattle's plan had worked to perfection thus far, Aveela knew. Prattle had been certain that these larger ships, fearing little from the smaller *Baubler*, would hardly pay her any heed when her sails showed on the horizon. And so the swift little *Baubler* had been able to move right up into range, and with this caravel's sails still fully exposed and full of wind.

Even now, with her rigging partially torn, the caravel crew hardly seemed panicked.

And why should they be? Aveela understood. Their ship was longer and higher than *Baubler*, thrice the weight and with a larger crew. That crew was ready for pirates, obviously, for they scrambled about on the deck, gathering their weapons and taking positions quite similar to those of *Baubler*'s crew.

"First volley!" Prattle called as *Baubler* bent back to port and glided parallel with the wounded caravel, keeping two to three hundred yards between them.

The archers didn't dip their arrows in the pitch — not at this distance. Aveela and the others bent back their bows and bent themselves backwards, launching their arrows high into the sky.

The caravel similarly responded, a volley at least as large — and similarly ineffective, with most of the arrows going each way splashing down harmlessly into the surf.

"Keep them busy and keep their eyes on us," Prattle remarked, walking up and down the line. He stopped when he got to Aveela.

"You see how unafraid they are?" he asked.

"They outnumber us, and with a ship much larger. If there's any ramming to be done, we're the ones sure to go under."

"And they think we are alone," Prattle explained, and he motioned off to the side, guiding Aveela's gaze with his own.

Even knowing where to look, it took the woman a long time to finally spot the powrie barrelboat, sliding like a giant shark through the swells. She moved south of their position, circling behind the caravel's stern.

"Their lookouts are scanning the horizon for sails," Prattle explained. "They can't believe that we'd dare come against them without a second boat. But where might it be?"

"So they think we're alone, and they think we're the fools," Aveela replied. "We've jammed their rigging, but it's not such a bad wound, nothing they can't repair and be on their way in short order."

"And they know our catapult isn't strong enough to do them any real harm," said Prattle, and even as he spoke, a ball of pitch went up into the air from the caravel, soaring their way, but landing harmlessly to the side, hitting the water with a great protesting hiss.

"And they know a hit or two from that bomber will put us under the waves," Prattle said with a laugh. "So we've got to keep moving and keep away, and from away, we can't really hurt them and can only hope that they don't sink us! They think we're the fools now, but I'm guessing that they'll be thinking differently in a few minutes." He ended with an exaggerated wink, and pulled a thick white paccaca root out of a pocket and tucked it into the side of his mouth, munching contentedly.

"What are you about, seascum?" came a cry from across the waves. Aveela, Prattle and the others watched a man in a ridiculously-decorated outfit, all frills and crisscrossing yellow bandoliers, with high feathered shoulders and a wide cap, ascend to the front rail of the caravel. "Your waters are south. You dare confront the might of Jacintha?"

Prattle gave another wink at Aveela and moved to the side, stepping up to a higher perch so that he would be visible to the distant Jacintha captain.

"Come on, then!" the distant commander cried. "You came for a fight, and a fight we'll give you! Bring your little jumper in and be done with it. And we'll be done with you, by Chezru! You've got no reefs to cover your run, pirate!"

Prattle munched his paccaca root and glanced at Aveela, grinning widely.

"They have us figured," the woman remarked.

"They think they do," Prattle corrected.

The captain of the caravel continued to shout, the archers on both ships continued to launch their mostly-ineffective volleys, and *Baubler* sidled back and forth across the waves, moving past the floating caravel, then turning about and coming across once more, and never moving the two ships closer together, despite the coaxing and prodding of the angry Jacintha captain. More bombs

soared out from the caravel, but *Baubler* was too nimble to be hit at this range.

The defiant caravel commander was still standing there on the rail, shouting curses, urging his archers on and shaking his fist in defiance, when the caravel lurched suddenly, water cresting and splashing all about the ship's port side. Men went tumbling across the deck, many going over the opposite rail; the captain grabbed desperately at the ropes but couldn't hold on and splashed into the rolling waters. Even the large catapult set aft creaked and groaned and pitched backwards, her throwing arm dislodging and crashing down to the deck.

"That would be our little friends," Prattle casually remarked.

With all the caravel crew's attention to port, toward *Baubler*, Besk and his barrelboat drove in hard against the starboard side, smashing amidship. Like all barrelboats, this one had an extended arm out front, an underwater ram, spiked and barbed.

The impact jolted all the powries and sent many flying from their seats, bouncing all about within the tub. But these were bloody cap dwarves, tougher than the stones of the Weathered Isles, as their ram and forward wall were tougher than the hull of any ship sailing the Mirianic.

Before they had even collected themselves and opened the hatches, they heard the desperate shouts of men in the water. Those sounds, of course, sent the bloody caps rushing for the hatch. A shout from Besk calmed them, though, and reminded them that they had a protocol to follow here, an order to their battle.

That design had Grave, as the youngest, going out last, and by the time he even got out onto the barrelboat deck, many of his kin were already up on the decks of the caravel, wailing away against the frightened and confused defenders. Other dwarves moved about the barrelboat deck with long gaff hooks, whacking and hooking any poor souls who ventured too near. Grave watched as one screaming and thrashing man was dragged up on the deck, a gaff buried deep into his shoulder. The young powrie couldn't help but compare the image to that of a large, hooked fish! A trio of powries fell over the human, hacking away with short and sturdy cleavers, and then, of course, dipping their berets in the spilling blood before the slopping seawater could wash it away.

The inexperienced Grave moved past them, taking off his dull beret to see if he might take a bit of the blood for his own. That was a measure of a powrie, after all, to dip his beret, his bloody cap, over and over again, to brighten it with the blood of many enemies. The berets, the bloody caps, were a powrie's source of pride and rank, and to some degree, of strength. For there was indeed an enchantment about those caps, a recipe as old as the Weathered Isles themselves. The more blood, the brighter the hue, and the more power – strength, toughness and even healing magic — the beret would lend to its wearer.

Grave thought he might begin that tinting process.

"Bah! Be gone, ye stinker!" one of the trio said to him, and he shoved Grave away so forcefully that the young dwarf nearly slipped into the water. "Ye go and get yer own!"

Grave came up on another dwarf who was swinging a long gaff pole out at a man flailing in the water. The pole splashed down harmlessly short of the mark.

"Bah!" the frustrated powrie snorted, and he turned to Grave. "Ye're wanting some blood, are ye? Then take me hand and hold me out so I can hook that dog and pull him in!"

Grave did as asked, securing himself as far out to the barrelboat's side as possible, and holding the gaffer at arms' length. The swimmer, however, seeing what was coming, had moved further out by then, and again, the hook hit only water.

"Bah!" the gaffer snorted again. "Good enough for ye, then! Sharks'll be coming in soon enough to eat ye!"

Grave slipped past, moving to the point of impact and the rope ladders. He grabbed on with strong hands and walked himself up to the caravel's tilting deck.

Just across the scene of chaos from him, *Baubler* had moved alongside, throwing her hooked planks, her crew already coming aboard, slicing through the meager remaining resistance.

Grave leaped all about, surveying the scene. Most of the defenders were already down, or had surrendered and were being herded to the forward tip of the leaning and sinking ship. All about Grave, his tough kin bent over dead or dying humans, dipping their caps. Many of the powries sported wounds, but they were a tougher lot than the sailors, and not a one complained.

"Ye go and dip yer hat wherever ye can find some blood."

The command surprised Grave, and he turned about to see Besk Morkis nodding at him. "It's why ye had to come out last," the powrie commander explained. "Ye got no hue, Mungo. Without some blood in yer cap, them human swords would've hurt ye bad, don't ye doubt! So go and get some blood. Next fight, I'll moved ye up in the line. Ye might even see a fight or two."

Grave scrambled across the deck. The caravel tilted even more, but few powries were caught off-guard or off-balance.

Powries were not easily knocked off balance.

Grave found no shortage of wounded, dying and dead upon whom to dip his cap, and each new donor made the beret shine just a bit more. He tried to stay near to Besk, though, for a pair of their human comrades, a huge man, more the size of an Alpinadoran barbarian than a typical Behrenese, and a young woman had come over, addressing Besk personally.

"Ye get all yer boys aboard and be quick about it," Besk instructed the pirate, speaking slowly and gesturing and motioning to help the pirate understand each point. Grave was glad of that, since his command of the southern tongue wasn't great at that point. "We hit her good and she's not to stay afloat for long."

"You give me an hour then to get the rest of the goods from her," the gigantic pirate replied.

"Bah! She won't last an hour," argued Besk. "Not if I get all me boys aboard and bailing."

"Just give me as long as you can."

"We'll take our booty from the flotsam," Besk added, and he walked away from the pair, toward Grave.

"Get yer dipping done, boy," Besk offered. "Ye're the last off the boat, but be quick about it."

The way he said that had the hairs on the back of Grave Mungo's neck itching.

"Last on, last off," Besk added, obviously seeing Grave's sudden curiosity. He paused and chuckled, a sound not unlike stone scraping against stone. "Don't ye worry, young one. We're not for leaving ye behind."

Besk moved to the side of the sinking ship and then over, and many of the powries followed him closely, while the others picked up their pace at dipping their berets and grabbing a few trinkets from the many bodies.

"A strange alliance, eh?"

The words surprised Grave, and even more so when he realized that they had been aimed at him. He turned to see the young human woman, the one who had been with the giant pirate when he was speaking with Besk.

"We caught the caravel off her guard," the woman went on. "They never anticipated that Cosinnida pirates would be working with powries."

Grave smiled and nodded, though he really hadn't understood every word. He had a general idea of what the woman might be talking about, though, for it seemed fairly obvious.

"Aveela Ashkar," the woman said, and it took Grave a moment to understand that to be her name. She extended her hand in greeting.

"Grave Mungo," he replied, and, not really knowing what to do with the extended hand, he just put his out beside hers. She took it at once and gave it a firm shake.

Grave looked at her curiously, and resisted his instinctive urge to crush her hand.

"It must get uncomfortable in that boat of yours," Aveela remarked.

"Uncom...." Grave shook his head, not knowing the Behrenese word.

"Hot," said Aveela.

"Aye," said Grave. "Hot, and...." He paused, then pinched his nose.

Aveela gave a laugh, then paused suddenly and looked all about. "Perhaps *Baubler*..."

Again, Grave scrunched up his face in confusion.

"*Baubler*," Aveela explained, pointing to her ship, and Grave nodded. "Perhaps it would be better for us all if one of your crew came aboard *Baubler*, to help us coordinate our attacks." She smiled and nodded eagerly.

Grave glanced back at the sailing ship, and he couldn't keep the look of honest intrigue from spreading across his hairy and leathery face.

"I can speak with Prattle," Aveela offered, and she pointed out the pirate leader. "Would you like to come aboard for a time?"

Grave brought his stubby hand up to stroke his chin. His gaze went from *Baubler* to the pirate captain, to Aveela, and when he looked back at the woman, to see her shrinking away, face crinkled in obvious disgust, he realized that his hand was covered in fresh blood from his beret dipping.

The powrie gave a little snort and dropped his hand to his side.

"Should I speak with him, Grave Mungo?" Aveela asked.

Grave was nodding before he even considered the implications, more at the woman's spunky attitude than at the proposition before him.

But why not? he thought. Certainly riding on the sailing ship would be a more agreeable time than scrunched up in the smelly barrelboat!

"Aye, talk to him," Grave said. "Ye make sure he asks for me, Grave Mungo!"

"I will do that," Aveela assured him, and she extended her hand again, and this time, the powrie took it and gave it a firm shake.

Grave looked around, only then realizing that he was alone among his kin still on the crippled ship. He tipped his beret at Aveela, then went to the side, dropping over quickly to the barrelboat deck, for even then, the hatch was starting to close.

"Taked ye long enough," Besk said to him with a laugh as he came scrambling back into the craft. "Now, ye get to yer place.

"All of ye to yer places!" Besk commanded, and it took Grave a moment to even recognize that his commander was speaking again in the powrie language.

"Quick, ye runts!" Besk roared. He turned to the controllers at the back of the boat. "Ye got them gears reversed?"

"Aye," the two dwarves said in unison.

"Then start yer pumping boys!" Besk called. "Yank us outa that busted boat!"

Grave sat there stunned. He knew that most of *Baubler*'s crew, including the giant captain, was still aboard the crippled ship. Hadn't Besk just assured the pirates that he'd give them some time?

Creaking wood brought the powrie from his thoughts and into the present, and he dutifully started pedaling.

The barrelboat ground backwards, pulling the crippled ship with it as the securing planks began to crack apart. Grave could imagine *Baubler*'s boarding planks tearing free and falling into the water. He could hear the shouts from the pirate crew and the prisoners alike, and could well imagine their confusion as they were dragged away from the one secure ship!

The dwarves pedaled with all their strength, towing the crippled caravel sidelong in the water, and then they broke free, suddenly, lurching back from the captured ship.

"Ha ha! She's rolling right over!" Besk shouted from the hatch tower. "Give us some room, ye fools, so we can get back in around the wreck!"

It all came clear to Grave, then. He wasn't soon to be feeling the wind on his face, riding aboard *Baubler*. Besk had betrayed the pirates, and now...

The barrelboat pulled back some more, and Besk ordered the controllers to reverse the gearing.

Then Besk shouted out his encouragement. "Come on, ye boys, push her hard. This one's not as heavy and won't take a hit!"

A few moments later, the barrelboat smashed into the side of *Baubler*, nearly splitting the light ship in two. Besk didn't order his crew out then to engage in battle.

There was no reason now.

They pulled the barrelboat back and sat back and waited as both ships broke apart and sank, leaving pirates and captives alike bobbing helplessly in the water.

Then the powries did come on deck, to claim their prizes, victims, trinkets and supplies alike.

Again Grave Mungo was one of the last to be allowed abovedeck, and by that point, any treading water near to the barrelboat had been dragged in and slaughtered.

The young powrie placed his hand firmly on his hips and stared at the carnage, and at the wasted opportunity. What gain had they really made this day, beyond the blood and a few coins and some more food?

Besk Morkis had made a clever deal here, one that would have served the powries well. And now he had thrown it away for the sake of one delicious kill.

"Grave!" came a shout from the water, and the powrie shielded the glare with one hand and followed the call to Aveela. She clung to a piece of wreckage.

Not so far behind her, Grave noted the passage of a dorsal fin.

"Grave Mungo!" the desperate woman cried.

"Ye know that one?" a powrie near Grave asked.

"Met her on the deck," Grave answered.

"Call her in, then," the powrie remarked.

Grave looked at him, puzzled.

"Go ahead," the older dwarf told him, and when he didn't immediately answer, or turn back to the water, he added, "What's her name, then?"

"Aveela," Grave said before he even considered the question.

"Aveela!" the other dwarf shouted, and in broken Behrenese, he added, "Come on, then! We'll take ye aboard!"

The woman had no choices here, made obvious by the horrified cry of one poor soul who happened to be in the way of a large and hungry shark. She began kicking her feet, propelling her toward the barrelboat.

"That's a good lass," the dwarf next to Grave remarked quietly. He looked Grave in the eye and offered an exaggerated wink.

Aveela moved closer.

"Shark behind ye!" Grave shouted as she came within a few feet of the

barrelboat. He wanted her to glance back, to look away. He didn't want her to see it coming.

The gaff hook chopped down hard, hitting the woman right on top of the head.

"Ha ha ha!" the other dwarf howled as the stuck woman flopped about in uncontrollable spasms.

The dwarf reeled her in.

"Lots o' bright blood for yer beret!" the dwarf offered to Grave.

Grave looked down at Aveela and viewed the twisted image on her face next to the curious and bright expression she had shown to him on the deck of the merchant caravel. The young powrie turned and walked away.

He moved to the front of the barrelboat and squatted there, looking out at the carnage, hearing the cries of terrified survivors who knew that the sharks would get them before any help could arrive. How pitiful they sounded, begging for mercy.

Mixing with those sounds came the laughter of Grave's powrie companions, many talking about the simple beauty of Besk's plan.

"The fat fool never thought we'd hit him like that!" one cried.

"Not in the first fight," said another. "Ah, the beauty!"

Grave was the only one among the dwarves who wasn't laughing. "No wonder then that we'll never get off our island," he muttered under his breath, taking care that none were close enough to hear. "No wonder then that we'll never have more than what we're knowing, scraping for food and living in the dirt."

With a final growl, Grave slapped himself across the thighs, rose up, and headed back for the hatch.

There lay Aveela, half on the boat and half off, her throat and chest ripped open.

Grave looked at her and remembered their exchange, and thought again of how much more agreeable it might have been to take a turn aboard the swift sailing ship.

And then he bent over and dipped his beret in her opened chest.

The End

Early versions of Abbot Greene,
ultimately discarded as too ornate

DemonWars

s k e t c h b o o k

by Ron Wagner

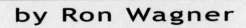

When artist Ron Wagner took on the assignment of illustrating the first *DemonWars* arc, he faced the daunting challenge of depicting a world that hadn't been visualized previously, but already was well defined in the minds of R.A. Salvatore's readers. The first few weeks of Wagner's time were dedicated exclusively to design work, establishing both the characters and settings.

"I've never had the opportunity to have that much design time. With most comics you're working on established characters, so anything you have to design you're doing on the fly," Wagner said. "It certainly helped me get a feel for the main characters, because they evolved over the entire design period."

The source material, of course, was the novel series, as well as consultations with Salvatore and Scott Ciencin. The resulting work, some of which appears on the following pages, speaks for itself.

"I'm grateful for the opportunity. I got to create things nobody else had touched before," Wagner said, adding that the villains of the series were some of his favorites. "I really enjoyed the powries and the giants. Seems like I'm more drawn to the bad guys, like always."

The Norse-inspired Chieftain Byggvir

A casual giant, along with
studies of Byggvir

Early versions of Elene, and a more literal
depiction of the demon Managarm

Various looks for
Andacanavar and Moira

Loose designs for Alpinadoran sailors and their village, eventually dubbed Hrungnir

ALPINADORAN SAILORS

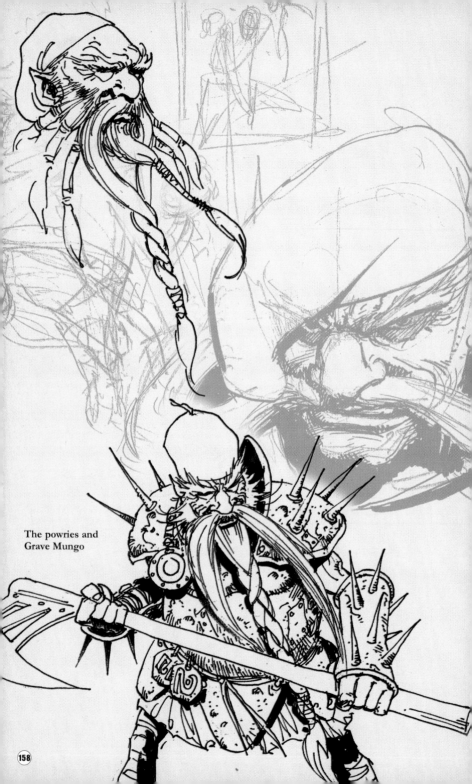

The powries and
Grave Mungo

CROSSGEN COMICS®
GRAPHIC NOVELS